HONEY, I LOVE

and other love poems

HONEY, I LOVE
and other love poems

by Eloise Greenfield
pictures by Diane and Leo Dillon

HarperCollins*Publishers*

The quotation used as epigraph is from
Teacup Full of Roses by Sharon Bell Mathis.
Copyright © 1972 by Sharon Bell Mathis.
All rights reserved. Reprinted by permission
of Viking Penguin Inc.

Honey, I Love and Other Love Poems
Text copyright © 1978 by Eloise Greenfield
Illustrations copyright © 1978 by Diane and Leo Dillon
All rights reserved. No part of this book may be used or
reproduced in any manner whatsoever without written permission
except in the case of brief quotations embodied in critical
articles and reviews. Manufactured in China.
For information address HarperCollins Children's Books,
a division of HarperCollins Publishers, 195 Broadway,
New York, NY 10007. Published simultaneously in
Canada by Fitzhenry & Whiteside Limited, Toronto. Published in
hardcover by Thomas Y. Crowell, New York.
www.harperchildrens.com

Library of Congress Cataloging-in-Publication Data
Greenfield, Eloise.
    Honey, I love and other love poems.
    Summary: Titles include "I Look Pretty," "Fun,"
"Riding on the Train," "Harriett Tubman," and "By Myself."
    ISBN 0-690-01334-5 — ISBN 0-06-443097-9 (pbk.)
    [American poetry—Afro-American authors.]
I. Dillon, Diane and Leo, ill.   II. Title.
PZ8.3G8Ho   77-2845
811'.5'4

19 20 SCP 45 44

For all of the people I have met over the years
who hold this book close to their hearts.
I am deeply grateful.

"...It's a love place. A real black love place."

—Sharon Bell Mathis,
Teacup Full of Roses

HONEY, I LOVE

I love
I love a lot of things, a whole lot of things
Like
My cousin comes to visit and you know he's from the South
'Cause every word he says just kind of slides out of his mouth
I like the way he whistles and I like the way he walks
But honey, let me tell you that I LOVE the way he talks
    I love the way my cousin talks
               and
The day is hot and icky and the sun sticks to my skin
Mr. Davis turns the hose on, everybody jumps right in
The water stings my stomach and I feel so nice and cool
Honey, let me tell you that I LOVE a flying pool
    I love to feel a flying pool
               and

Renee comes out to play and brings her doll without a dress
I make a dress with paper and that doll sure looks a mess
We laugh so loud and long and hard the doll falls to the ground
Honey, let me tell you that I LOVE the laughing sound

    I love to make the laughing sound

                and

My uncle's car is crowded and there's lots of food to eat
We're going down the country where the church folks like to meet
I'm looking out the window at the cows and trees outside
Honey, let me tell you that I LOVE to take a ride
I love to take a family ride

                and

My mama's on the sofa sewing buttons on my coat
I go and sit beside her, I'm through playing with my boat
I hold her arm and kiss it 'cause it feels so soft and warm
Honey, let me tell you that I LOVE my mama's arm

    I love to kiss my mama's arm

                and

It's not so late at night, but still I'm lying in my bed
I guess I need my rest, at least that's what my mama said
She told me not to cry 'cause she don't want to hear a peep
Honey, let me tell you I DON'T love to go to sleep

    I do not love to go to sleep

But I love
I love a lot of things, a whole lot of things
And honey,
I love you, too.

KEEPSAKE

Before Mrs. Williams died
She told Mr. Williams
When he gets home
To get a nickel out of her
Navy blue pocketbook
And give it to her
Sweet little gingerbread girl
That's me

I ain't never going to spend it

I LOOK PRETTY

Mama's shiny purple coat
Giant-sized shoulder bag to tote
Tall, tall shoes and pantyhose
Big straw hat with shiny bows
I look pretty
I float
I smile
I pose

WAY DOWN IN THE MUSIC

I get way down in the music
Down inside the music
I let it wake me
        take me
Spin me around and make me
Uh-get down

Inside the sound of the Jackson Five
Into the tune of Earth, Wind and Fire
Down in the bass where the beat comes from
Down in the horn and down in the drum
I get down
I get down

I get way down in the music
Down inside the music
I let it wake me
        take me
Spin me around and shake me
I get down, down
I get down

FUN

The pedal on our school piano squeaks
And one day Miss Allen stopped playing
And we stopped singing
And Mr. Cobb came with the skinny, silver can
And gave it a long, greasy drink
And the next day when we got ready to sing
Miss Allen smiled
       and blinked her eyes
       and plinked the piano
       and pushed the pedal
And the pedal said
       SQUEEEEEEEAK!
And we laughed
But Miss Allen didn't

ROPE RHYME

Get set, ready now, jump right in
Bounce and kick and giggle and spin
Listen to the rope when it hits the ground
Listen to that clappedy-slappedy sound
Jump right up when it tells you to
Come back down, whatever you do
Count to a hundred, count by ten
Start to count all over again
That's what jumping is all about
Get set, ready now,

        jump

           right

              out!

THINGS

Went to the corner
Walked in the store
Bought me some candy
Ain't got it no more
Ain't got it no more

Went to the beach
Played on the shore
Built me a sandhouse
Ain't got it no more
Ain't got it no more

Went to the kitchen
Lay down on the floor
Made me a poem
Still got it
Still got it

I hear
ruggety-ruggety
squeakety-squeakety
rumbledy-rumbledy
woonh, WOONH!
Wil — ming — tonnnnnnn

I feel
my leg jiggling
my bottom bouncing
my shoulders shaking
my head rolling
I'm getting s l e

                    e

                       e

                          e

                             p y

AUNT ROBERTA

What do people think about
When they sit and dream
All wrapped up in quiet
   and old sweaters
And don't even hear me 'til I
Slam the door?

:GGIE

 summertime
d Reggie doesn't live here anymore
 lives across the street
ends his time with the round ball
mp, turn, shoot
rough the hoop
ends his time with arguments
and sweaty friends
d not with us
's moved away
mes here just to eat and sleep
and sometimes pat my head
en goes back home
 run and dribble and jump and stretch
d stretch
d shoot
inks he's Kareem
d not my brother

LESSIE

When my friend Lessie runs she runs so fast
I can hardly see her feet touch the ground
She runs faster than a leaf flies
She pushes her knees up and down, up and down
She closes her hands and swings her arms
She opens her mouth and tastes the wind
Her coat flies out behind her

When Lessie runs she runs so fast that
Sometimes she falls down
But she gets right up and brushes her knees
And runs again as fast as she can
Past red houses
     and parked cars
     and bicycles
     and sleeping dogs
     and cartwheeling girls
     and wrestling boys
     and Mr. Taylor's record store
All the way to the corner
To meet her mama

MOOCHIE

Moochie likes to keep on playing
That same old silly game
Peeka   Boo!
Peeka   Boo!

I get tired of it
But it makes her laugh
And every time she laughs
She gets the hiccups
And every time she gets the hiccups
I laugh

HARRIET TUBMAN

Harriet Tubman didn't take no stuff
Wasn't scared of nothing neither
Didn't come in this world to be no slave
And wasn't going to stay one either

"Farewell!" she sang to her friends one night
She was mighty sad to leave 'em
But she ran away that dark, hot night
Ran looking for her freedom

She ran to the woods and she ran through the woods
With the slave catchers right behind her
And she kept on going till she got to the North
Where those mean men couldn't find her

Nineteen times she went back South
To get three hundred others
She ran for her freedom nineteen times
To save Black sisters and brothers
Harriet Tubman didn't take no stuff
Wasn't scared of nothing neither
Didn't come in this world to be no slave
And didn't stay one either

And didn't stay one either

BY MYSELF

When I'm by myself
And I close my eyes
I'm a twin
I'm a dimple in a chin
I'm a room full of toys
I'm a squeaky noise
I'm a gospel song
I'm a gong
I'm a leaf turning red
I'm a loaf of brown bread
I'm a whatever I want to be
An anything I care to be
And when I open my eyes
What I care to be
Is me

LOVE DON'T MEAN

Love don't mean all that kissing
Like on television
Love means Daddy
Saying keep your mama company
   till I get back
And me doing it

I love
I love a lot of things
A whole lot of things
And honey,
I love ME, too

Eloise Greenfield's first collection of poems clearly reflects her deepest aim in all her children's books—"to give [them] words to love, to grow on." Ms. Greenfield's biographies and fiction for children have received numerous awards for their excellence, including the first Carter G. Woodson Award for her *Rosa Parks* and the Jane Addams Children's Book Award for *Paul Robeson*. She has received a special citation from the Council on Interracial Books for Children, for her "outstanding and exemplary contributions in . . . children's literature."

The picture-book illustrations of Diane and Leo Dillon have won them the prized Caldecott Award for two consecutive years. They bring years of study to their book design and illustration, and they refuse to be restricted to any one style or technique. Among the memorable picture books to their credit is *Song of the Boat* by Lorenz Graham, an A.L.A. Notable Children's Book.